THE CREEPY CAMPOUT Girl Scout MYSTERY

First Edition ©2015 Carole Marsh/Gallopade International/Peachtree City, GA
Current Edition ©November 2017
Ebook edition ©2015
All rights reserved.
Manufactured in Peachtree City, GA

Carole Marsh Mysteries™ and its skull colophon are the property of Carole Marsh and
Gallopade International.

Published by Gallopade International/Carole Marsh Books. Printed in the United States
of America.

Managing Editor: Janice Baker
Assistant Editor: Susan Walworth
Cover Design: Randolyn Friedlander
Content Design: Randolyn Friedlander

*Gallopade is proud to be a member and supporter of these educational
organizations and associations:*

**American Booksellers Association
American Library Association
International Reading Association
National Association for Gifted Children
The National School Supply and Equipment Association
The National Council for the Social Studies
Museum Store Association
Association of Partners for Public Lands
Association of Booksellers for Children
Association for the Study of African American Life and History
National Alliance of Black School Educators**

Dear Readers,

Seriously, what's more fun than camping out?! Sleeping under the stars? Roasting hot dogs over an open fire? Biting into ooey-gooey s'mores? Telling ghost stories in the moonlight? Waking up to a magnificent sunrise coming over the horizon?

When you read this book, you'll join a group of Girl Scouts on a spooky, spirited romp in the great outdoors. Besides having loads of fun, the girls in this story learn a lot about independence, trying new things, getting along with others, and surviving when away from the comforts of home.

You'll learn those same lessons when you're camping out. And be assured that those experiences will turn into valuable nuggets of wisdom you and every other Girl Scout will take with you along the journey of life!

So, settle into a comfortable chair and join our Girl Scouts as they get outside, get to work, get challenged, and giggle a LOT in the Creepy Campout Mystery!

You go, girls!

Carole Marsh

TABLE OF CONTENTS

1

I CAN! OR CAN I?

Ella watched her friend Kiara waddle down the wooded path to the campsite like a colorful, lumpy marshmallow with legs. Tucked under one arm was her green and yellow, dots and daisies sleeping bag. Her favorite pillow in its satin fuchsia pillowcase bulged beneath her other arm. An overstuffed Girl Scout backpack covered with hearts and stars bounced on her back like a loose turtle shell.

"Hurry up, Ella!" Kiara yelled over her shoulder. "Two by two is the Girl Scout thing to do!"

"Coming, Kiara!" Ella yelled, remembering their troop leader's speech on how important it was to "buddy up" when camping. Ella hoped she would be a good buddy on this camping trip. On her first campout last year as a Daisy, things hadn't gone so well. In the middle of the night, she had a vivid nightmare of a horrendous grizzly bear clawing its way into her tent. Her screams woke the entire troop, including her frazzled leader who promptly called her grandparents Mimi and Papa to come and pick her up.

"Need some help?" Papa asked tenderly, slipping the strap of Ella's Girl Scout backpack over her shoulder.

Jarred from her disturbing thoughts, Ella worried this year might be a repeat performance. Hadn't Mimi and Papa booked a hotel room thirty minutes away "just in case"?

"I'll be fine," Ella assured Papa. She patted her backpack. "See? I chose a pack covered in peace signs to remind me to have a peaceful camping trip. Besides, I'm a Brownie this time!"

"Yes, you are," Mimi said as she admired the Brownie pin on Ella's shirt. "I hadn't noticed before that your pin's not upside down!"

When Ella received her pin a few weeks earlier during her investiture ceremony, she had to wear it upside down until she did a good deed. "I picked up trash on my neighborhood playground," she explained, puffing out her chest with pride. "Our troop leader said we could wear our pins even when we're not wearing our uniforms, so that everyone will know we're Brownies."

"That's a great idea," Mimi said, "and I'm sure you'll do many more good deeds here at Camp Poplar. You'll probably even earn some badges. Did you remember your sash?"

"Of course, Mimi," Ella replied. "It's in my backpack. Remember, we're having an award ceremony on the last day." She giggled. "No sash, no place for badges. I'd be up the creek without a paddle!"

Papa groaned. "You've been around Mimi too much. You're using her favorite idiom!"

Mimi smiled and continued her pep talk. "There's no telling what adventures await around that bend in the trail!"

Ella glanced back at the trail where Kiara had already disappeared. An afternoon thunderstorm had left the ground soggy. Now, an eerie mist rose from it like ghostly spirits. "Or maybe mysteries?" she said expectantly. "I might stumble on some great ideas for your next book."

"You leave the mysteries to your famous mystery-writing grandmother," Papa said as he shifted his black cowboy hat on his head. "Mysteries lead to danger. You stay safe!"

Mimi winked. "She'll stay safe. Two girls here at Camp Poplar will make sure of that!"

Ella knew Mimi was talking about her sister Avery, a Girl Scout Junior, and her first cousin Christina, one of the camp counselors. Ella couldn't deny she was glad to have them close by, but she really didn't know how helpful Avery would be. Since becoming best friends with Pari, a new girl in her troop, she was acting different.

Pari had ridden with them to camp. As soon as Papa stopped his truck, Pari grabbed her gear, waved goodbye, and raced to the campsite yelling, "Last one in camp is a baby Brownie!" Instead of waiting for Ella, Avery had giggled and chased after her.

Mimi brushed wisps of Ella's blonde hair off her face and stamped a kiss in the center of her forehead. Ella rolled her eyes, knowing that her grandmother's bright red lip prints were glowing on her head like a neon sign. "Got to go," she said, giving each of her grandparents a hug and waving goodbye bravely. "See you in a few!"

Hearing the excited squeals and chatter of her fellow Girl Scouts coming from the camp, she only hoped "a few" meant days and not hours. To encourage herself she chanted in rhythm with her footsteps on the path, "I can do this! I can do this! I can do this!"

But when she heard Papa's big truck tires crunching on the gravel as they pulled onto the main road, another pesky little voice in her head whispered, "Can I do this? Can I do this? Can I do this?"

It was too late to change her mind. There was no turning back now!

BROWNIE OR MUD PIE?

Ella tramped along the path, her confidence growing with every step. Sunset rays broke through the trees and speared the ground. At the end of one spear, just off the trail, Ella spotted a flower in a small clearing so orange it seemed to be on fire.

"It's a butterflyweed," she whispered. She recognized the flower from a book her troop had read about native wildflowers. Her first thought was to pick it and show it to Mrs. Scott, her troop leader. But Ella knew better. Picking wildflowers was not the Girl Scout way. She knew that without flowers, the plant couldn't make seeds to make more plants.

Ella had a better idea. She plopped all her gear in a heap, and dug for the camera in her backpack. Her rummaging fingers touched her sash and she smiled. "This flower picture should help me earn a badge!"

Forgetting her nervousness, she stepped gingerly off the trail, lured by the flower's beauty. Focusing her camera lens, she gasped. "Oh," she murmured, "there's even a monarch butterfly feeding on it!" She spoke to the butterfly like it could understand her. "Stay put, please," she coaxed. "I just need to get your picture. I promise it won't hurt a bit!"

Ella slid her feet in tiny steps through the smoky fog that hugged the ground like a fallen cloud. She tried not to make any moves that would frighten the delicate creature. But just as she was about to take the picture, she tumbled face first into the wet, muddy ground.

"EEYOWWWWW!" she yelled. Pain raced up her left leg. Something had grabbed her ankle. Was it claws or teeth? Ella's racing imagination begged for an answer.

She pulled her face out of the mud just enough to suck in a trembling breath. If she moved, the bear, or monster, or whatever had nabbed her, might pull her away to its forest lair. *Is it better to play dead or make a run for it?* she wondered. *What would Girl Scout founder Juliette Gordon Low do in a situation like this?*

Ella didn't remember any guidelines on how to wrestle bears or outsmart monsters in her Brownie handbook, which she'd already read twice. But she did know she'd already broken two of the rules: go everywhere two by two and stay on the trail. Two strikes and she hadn't even made it to camp yet! Didn't Avery, Kiara, or someone–anyone–realize she wasn't there? "Why aren't they looking for me?" she fretted.

Right on cue, someone called her name in the distance. "Ella?" echoed through the trees. It was Mrs. Scott calling roll. *If I answer, I might rile whatever's holding my ankle,* she thought.

Before making her move, Ella waited a few seconds that seemed like hours. Slowly, she pushed up on her elbows. When nothing happened, she turned her head like an old turtle to the left, and then to the right. She saw nothing.

Ella rolled onto her back and pulled her legs toward her. Her right leg came easily, but her left leg, hurting like crazy, wouldn't budge. Ella sat up to find a lasso of briars wound firmly around her ankle.

"WHEW!" she exclaimed, relieved that it was only briars and not a bear. But her relief was short-lived. She rested her cheek in her hand to watch the last of the sunlight drain from the sky like dirty dishwater from a sink. To her horror, she felt something cold and slimy plastered to her face! Images of bloodsucking worms she'd seen in Avery's science book flashed through her mind. "Bloodsucker!" she yelled.

Ella wriggled her tangled leg free and raced through the woods, dodging trees in the dim light like an Olympic skier in a slalom event. Just when she thought her lungs would burst, Ella spotted the twinkling lanterns of camp at the bottom of the hill.

"Help me!!!" she hollered to her fellow campers. Frightened Girl Scout faces peered into the darkness as Ella's foot hit a slick patch of red clay that shot her down the hill like a greasy pig on a slip-n-slide. She skidded to a stop in a circle of girls.

"Help me, pleeeaase!" she pleaded. But her pleas were met with looks of puzzlement and panic. Girl Scouts were supposed to "be prepared," but nothing had prepared them for this. Should they help, or run from this unrecognizable creature with its wild tangle of blond hair, mud-caked face, and clothes mottled with muck?

"Mrs. Scott!" one girl called. "You better get over here!"

Kiara cautiously shined her flashlight in Ella's face. "Ella?" she asked. "Is that you?"

"Of c-c-course, it's m-m-me," Ella stuttered, pointing to the thing plastered to her cheek. "I'v-v-ve got a blood s-s-sucker on my f-f-face!"

Kiara jumped back instinctively. "A what?"

"It's a b-b-blood s-s-sucker," Ella said again. "A leech! Get it off p-p-please!"

19

"There's nothing in my Brownie book about pulling off leeches," Kiara said, wrinkling her face in disgust. "I love you, friend, but no way am I touching that thing!"

Avery pushed her way through the ring of gawking girls with Mrs. Scott close behind her. "Ella!" Avery said, shocked at her sister's appearance. "Are you OK?"

Mrs. Scott calmly ordered Kiara, "Please call Mrs. Dunn to come over here. And go get a camp counselor too."

"Just get it off!" Ella screamed, pointing to the gooey glob on her cheek. "GET THE LEECH OFF MY FACE!"

"Leech?" Mrs. Scott asked.

Avery carefully pulled the slimy, mud-caked object off Ella's cheek. "That's no leech," she remarked. "It's a leaf!"

The circle of girls burst into laughter. Ella's face burned under its muddy crust.

Mrs. Scott gave the Girl Scout quiet sign by raising her right hand as she patted Ella's head consolingly with her left. The girls obediently raised their right hands and hushed. Kiara soon returned with Mrs. Dunn and the counselor. They carried a first-aid kit with them. Ella was thankful to hear the familiar voice of her cousin Christina.

"What in the world?!" Christina exclaimed.

Mrs. Scott moved Ella's hair off her face and exposed a bright red mark. "Oh, my goodness!" she cried. "She's bleeding!"

Christina leaned in for a closer look. "No worries," she said. "I'd recognize that shade of red anywhere. Looks like Mimi gave you a good luck kiss!"

Ella nodded sheepishly.

Relieved there was no injury to Ella's face, Mrs. Scott clapped her hands with authority and picked up her Kaper chart, which listed each girl's camp chores. "OK, girls," she said. "Let's finish getting those tents up!"

Christina helped Ella to her feet. "Let's get you cleaned up," she said. "We'll have you looking like a Brownie instead of a mud pie in no time."

Avery looked at her little sister sympathetically. "I should have walked to camp with you," she said. "Then, none of this would've happened."

Avery's friend Pari flipped her long, glossy black hair off her shoulders. "It's not your fault, Avery," she said. Then, looking straight at Ella, she muttered, "Maybe some Brownies are ready for a campout, and some are not."

Tears formed muddy rivers on Ella's dirty cheeks. She hoped no one could see them in the dark. Her confidence that this would be her first successful camping trip was disappearing faster than s'mores around a campfire. And she had a bad feeling that things would only get worse—much worse.

3

SASH DASH

A warm shower would have been nice. But a cold bath in the camp's bathroom sink was better than the alternative—a dip in Cryptic Lake. The mysterious lake was known for the thick blanket of fog that often covered it. But its mysteriousness didn't end with just fog.

Like generations of Girl Scouts, Ella had heard the legend of Tic-Lic, a lizard-like creature that supposedly lived in the lake. With a snaking neck the length of a school bus and a tubby body, the creature was said to change color like a chameleon. In the murky lake, its iridescent scales allowed it to slip unseen through the water. On land, the scales turned to mottled shades of brown and green as Tic-Lic waddled on stubby legs with wide, webbed feet ending in dagger claws.

Tic-Lic's long, clammy, purple tongue was described as his most distinguishing feature. At its tip, the tongue split into wiggling tentacles that resembled a feather duster. The legend claimed that each night, Tic-Lic lumbered into camp and used his tongue to tickle the toes of every sleeping Girl Scout.

Ella shuddered at the thought of slimy lizard saliva on her toes, but she shook the worry of a mythical monster out of her thoughts. She had something worse to worry about—facing the girls who'd seen her make a fool of herself.

Dressed in clean jeans and her favorite green sweatshirt, Ella entered the circle of tents. Girls clustered in an excited huddle around the fire pit where a tiny teepee of twigs had caught fire. Several Junior Girl Scouts added larger sticks to the fire, while Brownies watched sparks soar into the night sky like fireflies set free from a jar.

Ella was glad Kiara was the only one who noticed her. "Yay!" Kiara said. "You're looking like your old clean self. The camp counselors found your gear on the trail, and

I got all our stuff put away in the tent. Guess who our roomies are?"

"Who?" Ella asked as she plopped down on a log beside Kiara.

"Avery and Pari!" Kiara exclaimed.

"Great," Ella groaned. Before Avery became best friends with Pari, Ella would have been thrilled to bunk with her sister. Now, Ella was second fiddle.

Kiara clapped her hands rapidly while bouncing up and down on the log. "I can't wait!" she said. "We're roasting hot dogs. And," she added, waving her hand at the long table of food like a game show hostess, "Dat da da daaaaaa—s'mores!"

"Calm down," Ella said. "You act like you've never eaten a hot dog or s'mores."

"I have eaten a hot dog, but I've never roasted one on a fire!" Kiara said. "And I've never made s'mores! You know this is my first campout."

Ella shook her head and shuddered. "I hate s'mores," she confessed, "but I do like to make them."

The roaring fire flicked sharp tongues of flame into the night sky like an angry dragon when Avery and Pari stepped out of the darkness and into the circle. Chattering like birds, they perched on the log beside Ella and Kiara.

"Look," Avery whispered to Ella. She wriggled her fingers in the firelight. Her nails, each a different color, were coated in glitter polish. "Pari did my nails," she said.

Ella's mouth curled in a smirk as she rolled her eyes and shook her head. "How'd your nails get so long so fast?"

"They're fake," Avery explained. "Glued right on top of my real nails. This look is really in style right now."

Ella examined her own dirt-encrusted nails and struggled to think of a disapproving comment. "Well, I think they look like...like...a witch stuck her hands in a pot of glitter."

"You're just jealous!" Avery said hastily. "Pari's right. You do act like a baby. That's why she didn't want us in the same tent as you! Too bad Mrs. Scott made us!"

Ella's cheeks glowed with embarrassment. Before Ella could respond to her sister, Mrs. Scott belted out a warning. "Be careful with these," she said, handing the girls the roasting sticks they had made at their last meeting. "The tips are sharp!"

"Isn't mine pretty?" Pari boasted. Like Avery's nails, the wooden handle was covered in glitter. Pastel colored streamers flowed from the end.

"That's beautiful," Kiara agreed, eyeing the simple red and blue handle on her roasting stick. "I wish I'd done mine like that."

"Maybe when you're a Junior Girl Scout, you can make one as pretty as mine," Pari said.

Ella stabbed a hot dog angrily with her plain green roasting stick. "I like yours the way it is," she told Kiara loudly enough for Pari to hear.

"Thanks, friend," Kiara said, spearing her own hot dog and eagerly plunging it into the fire. It quickly became a flaming comet.

"Blow it out!" Ella yelled. Both girls huffed and puffed. "Poor thing. It looks sunburned," Kiara said as she placed the steaming hot dog in a bun. She opened her mouth wide for a huge chomp, but Ella yelled, "WAIT!"

"What?!" Kiara asked. A disgusted look spread across her face. "Did you spit on it when we blew it out?"

"No," Ella said with a giggle, "not on purpose anyway! I just want to get a picture of you eating your first fire-roasted hot dog."

When Ella snapped the picture, Kiara took a bite of her hot dog, rolled her eyes, and rubbed her tummy. "Mmmmm," she hummed. "I love campfire cooking!"

"You better slow down," Ella warned as Kiara polished off her third hot dog before Ella finished her first. "Those dogs may be barking in your stomach later tonight!"

Kiara grinned and held her roasting stick like a queen's royal scepter. "Bring on the marshmallows!" she commanded.

Mrs. Scott vetoed Kiara's command. "Before we roast marshmallows," she said, "I want you to walk to your tents for your sashes. Be very careful moving around the fire. Then, wear your sashes back to the campfire circle. Be ready to tell about the Girl Scout Journey you're on and the badges you'd like to earn on this camping trip. The first group back will be the first one to make s'mores."

The girls carefully maneuvered around the fire and headed to their tents. Kiara quickly outpaced Ella and reached the tent first. Avery was close behind them.

When Ella threw back the tent flap to go inside, a shocking sight greeted her. Her sleeping bag, pillow, and clothes lay helter skelter around one side of the tent. "I thought you put my stuff away!" she said accusingly to Kiara, who stood with her mouth open in surprise.

"But I...I...I...did," Kiara stammered. "I put our stuff away neatly and laid our sleeping bags out beside each other. See? My stuff is a mess too!"

Ella turned to Avery, who looked as surprised as Kiara. That's when Ella noticed the startling contrast of the other side of the tent. Everything there was neatly stowed, except the glitter nail polish Pari had used on Avery's nails.

"I see," Ella huffed. "We've been pranked! What a nasty thing to do!"

Ella and Kiara searched for their sashes in the mess. Kiara yelled, "Found it!" But then she cupped her fist on her chin and tapped her cheek with her pointer finger. "But," she said, "I can't find my cookies. My grandma decorated the bag with hearts. Wait a minute—did I eat them already?"

Ella, rummaging through her scattered belongings, finally spotted her backpack. "That's where my sash was," she said. "It's gotta be in there!" But when she turned the backpack upside down, it was empty. "Somebody's stolen my sash!" she cried.

4

TO TELL OR
NOT TO TELL?

"You have to tell Mrs. Scott," Kiara told Ella as they walked back to the campfire where girls were already roasting marshmallows and sharing their camp goals.

"No way," Ella replied. "If she thinks I'm in trouble that I can't handle, she'll call my grandparents for sure. If she thinks I lost my sash, she'll think I'm an irresponsible kid."

Ella stopped and stood tall. "You know," she remarked, "solving mysteries is in my blood. I'll take the challenge of the missing sash. I'll have my sash back for the final ceremony. You wait and see!"

"What do you mean?" Kiara asked.

"Don't you get it?" Ella asked. "Pari doesn't want us in her tent. She probably took my sash hoping I'd get so upset I'd want to go home. And where was she when we went to the tent? She had suspiciously disappeared from the campfire circle. That's probably when she slipped away to wreck the tent and take my sash."

Ella shook her blond head. "I won't let her get away with it. I'll prove she did it! Then maybe she'll be the one who gets sent home."

"But why would she take your sash and not take mine?" Kiara asked, tracing her badges with her finger.

"I'm not sure," Ella said. "Maybe she didn't find your sash."

"Don't forget about my missing cookies," Kiara said. "Maybe she took those instead of my sash."

"But she likes you," Ella said. "She likes anyone who thinks she's 'all that'."

Ella focused her camera on the ring of Girl Scouts around the campfire and snapped a picture. "It's me she wants out of the picture," she mumbled.

"Pari is creative and she has really pretty hair, but I don't like her more than you," Kiara said. "You're my best friend. Can I help you solve the mystery?"

"Sure," Ella said. "We already have a motive. All we need are clues that will lead us to where she hid the sash."

"First," Kiara said, "we need to find out where Pari is now. And by the way, where's Avery?"

"When we left the tent, Avery was going to look for Pari," Ella answered. "I hope she finds her somewhere feeling guilty about what she did."

Ella's camera screen threw an unearthly green glow across her face as she thumbed through her pictures. She snickered. "There's the blurry picture I almost got of the butterfly on the butterflyweed."

"Aren't you afraid Avery will tell Mrs. Scott or the other adults about what happened?"

Kiara asked. "Or do you think Avery helped Pari do it?"

"Avery has changed," Ella said, "but I don't believe she would do something like that. Besides, she probably knows I suspect Pari. She wouldn't want her best friend to get in trouble. So, no, I don't think she'll tell anyone."

"Heyyyy!" Ella exclaimed as she continued to stare at the camera screen. "Look at this!"

"That's the picture you made of me eating the hot dog," Kiara said, poking her head into the screen's glow. "Good shot! Will you send it to me?"

"Sure," Ella answered. She pointed to a corner of the photo and zoomed the image in closer. "But look in the background," she said. "See those shadowy figures walking away from the campfire? One of them must be Pari sneaking away to wreck our tent. But who is the other one?"

5

SLEEP TIGHT, TIC-LIC

Avery and Pari slipped back into the campfire circle just as Ella and Kiara stood before everyone to share their camp goals. Ella was relieved Mrs. Scott didn't notice she wasn't wearing her sash.

Afterward, Kiara was eager to make s'mores. Ella pushed six fluffy marshmallows onto her roasting stick and held them over the fire until they flamed like a tiki torch. She waved the stick back and forth to extinguish the flames and then offered them to her friend.

"Ooey, goooey!" Kiara said. She pulled off three white globs, placed them on top of graham cracker and chocolate squares, and smooshed another graham cracker on top. "Now that's what I call a sandwich!" she said.

"Can I have the other three marshmallows?" Pari begged. "Mine fell in the fire."

Ella held her stick tightly.

"You know you don't even like them, Ella!" Avery said. "Give them to Pari."

"I'm eating these," Ella declared firmly.

"Oh, yeah?" Avery said, pulling one of the marshmallows off Ella's stick. "Then open wide."

Avery stuffed the marshmallow into Ella's mouth.

"Ewww!" Ella finally managed to say. "It's crunchy!"

"Marshmallows are not crunchy!" Avery said. "That's just ridiculous."

"This one is," Ella answered, spitting something hard out in her hand and looking at it closely.

"Gross!!" she said, spitting furiously on the ground. "Disgusting! Your fake fingernail came off in my marshmallow!"

Avery and Pari looked at each other and burst into laughter. "Now that's what I call finger food!" Pari cried.

After the campfire finally died, the Girl Scouts in charge of caring for it scattered the ashes and sprinkled them with water. "Time for bed!" Mrs. Scott announced.

When they were in their tent, Pari told Ella sarcastically, "You know, I'm sorry your stuff got messed up."

"Apology accepted," Ella said. But then she whirled around to stare right into Pari's brown eyes. "GIVE ME BACK MY SASH!" Ella demanded.

"I wasn't apologizing," Pari said, rocking her head sassily. "I did not mess with your stuff, and I do not have your silly sash! It's not my fault you're a Brownie baby and can't take care of your things. Why don't you call your Mimi and Papa to come and get you?"

"I'm sure you'd like that," Ella replied. "But first I have to prove you took my sash!"

"Get off her back, Ella!" Avery ordered. "Why do you think Pari did it?"

"First, she doesn't want me in the tent," Ella said, hurt that her sister was taking Pari's side. "Second, she keeps calling me a baby Brownie. And third, I have a picture of her sneaking away from the campfire."

Ella passed her camera to Avery. "This picture was made about the same time Pari disappeared," Ella said. "I'm sure she's one of the shadowy figures in this picture. I can make out her long hair. And it looks like she had the help of a friend."

Avery looked at Pari, confused. "This does kinda look like you," she admitted.

"It probably is me," Pari announced. "You know the rule is to leave the campfire circle silently on the outside of the ring of logs. I had to use the latrine!"

"The la-what?" Kiara asked.

"You little kids don't even know the names of things," Pari said. "Latrine is the camp word for bathroom."

"Pari's telling the truth," Avery said. "When I went looking for her, she was in the latrine."

"Maybe she stopped by the tent on her way there," Ella suggested. "Or maybe her friend did."

"The only friend I have at this camp is Avery," Pari said angrily.

"Then who were you talking to?" Ella fired back.

Pari snatched the camera from Avery's hands and examined the picture. "It must be that lady," she said.

"What lady?" Avery asked.

"There was a lady standing outside the campfire circle," Pari said. "She nearly scared me to death when she stepped out from behind a tree. I hadn't seen her in the camp before. She was yakking on and on about how wonderful it is to be a Girl Scout and how she wished she could be a young girl again. When my flashlight shined on her boots, they were glistening with wet mud. And she was carrying a metal box."

"Maybe she was a ghost in muddy boots," Ella said sarcastically. "Was she wearing a long white gown? Could you see right through her?"

"Stop teasing," Kiara said. "You're gonna give me nightmares!"

Avery sighed and pulled her long blonde hair into a ponytail. "We're not gonna figure anything out tonight, so why don't we agree to disagree and get some sleep."

Ella looked at the mess on their side of the tent and huffed. "Some of us have to clean up before we have a place to sleep," she said.

"Yeah," Kiara agreed. "We need some real Brownies to clean up this mess."

"What do you mean?" Pari asked. "Aren't you two real Brownies?"

"I mean the little elves who sneak in and clean your house," Kiara explained. "They're like fairies."

"Pari doesn't know about Brownies," Avery said. "She lived in India with her mom when she was little. She's only been a Girl Scout since moving to the United States to live with her father."

Pari had a faraway look in her eyes. "My grandmother in India told me that my name means fairy," she said. "I guess I would've been a good Brownie."

"You still can be," Avery said. "Let's all work together!"

"That could count as our good deeds for the day," Kiara suggested, clapping her hands rapidly.

The girls buzzed around the tent, picking up and straightening, and soon all was in order.

"Let's jump in our jammies," Avery said. "The last one zipped in her sleeping bag has to catch a frog by the end of camp!"

Zip! Zip! Avery and Pari quickly snuggled in their sleeping bags.

Kiara pulled her sleeping bag on like a pair of puffy pants and flopped on the tent floor. Zip! "Ouch!!" she yelled. "There's a rock under our tent!" She wriggled like a giant purple caterpillar to a comfortable spot.

In her rush, Ella put her pajama top on backwards. "Of course, I'd be last," she moaned, turning her top around and finally zipping into her sleeping bag.

"I hope you catch a big, slimy frog covered with warts!" Pari said.

"If you want to keep Tic-Lic from tickling your toes tonight, you have to do this," Avery warned. She kissed her sleeping bag's zipper pull and said, "Sleep tight, Tic-Lic!"

"Sleep tight, Tic-Lic," the girls echoed.

Worried about her sash, Ella almost hoped Tic-Lic would come and tickle her toes. She needed a good laugh.

6

SOUND OF SILENCE

BANG! BANG! BAM! BANG! Ella bolted upright and held her breath. Was Tic-Lic in the camp? Was he headed her way? A scream began clawing its way up her throat.

"Come and get it!" Mrs. Scott yelled.

Ella exhaled.

"Why does she bang on that pot to wake us up?" Avery groaned and stretched in her puffy sleeping bag covered with yellow and white daisies.

Kiara yawned like a sleepy lion. "I hope she's cooking something in that pot. I'm starving!"

Ella patted her sleeping bag and grinned. The dim morning light glowed through the tent's pink fabric. *I made it!* she thought. She raised her arms in a triumphant stretch. "I had crazy dreams about naughty Brownies and mysterious, shadowy figures wearing my sash, but—I SURVIVED MY FIRST NIGHT AT CAMP!"

Seeing her tent mates stirring, Pari winked at Avery and sniffed the air. "Is that bacon?"

"Smells like bacon to me," Avery agreed.

"Bacon would be soooo good!" Kiara said. "Did I mention that I'm starving?"

Ella and Kiara unzipped their sleeping bags in unison—Zip! But when each of them slung their bags open they were met with a horrific sight—big, hairy black spiders!

"Yiiiiiikes!" Ella screamed, kicking her feet frantically to get away from her bag.

"Help me!" Kiara yelled, clapping her hands and jumping up and down.

Together, the girls charged toward the tent flap that Avery had already unzipped. BOING!! They face-planted into a wall of plastic wrap and bounced back onto the tent floor.

"We're trapped!" Kiara cried. "The spiders are gonna get us!"

"We need scissors!" Ella begged.

Pari and Avery laughed like hyenas. "I knew they'd fall for it," Pari said. "That was worth the work of winding that plastic wrap around the tent!"

Still breathing heavily, Ella looked closely at the spiders. They hadn't moved at all. One was even upside down on its back. "Wait a minute," she said, poking at one. She hesitantly picked it up by one hairy leg. "Rubber spiders," she murmured. She propped up on her elbows and glared at Pari. "I should have known you had other mean tricks up your sleeve."

"Actually, that was my idea," Avery admitted. "As soon as you two were asleep we sealed the door and put the spiders in your sleeping bags. I planned it weeks ago. It wouldn't be camp without pranks, and those are classics!"

"OK, you got us," Kiara said. "But I'm glad I landed on my pillow instead of that rock."

A smile tugged at the corners of Ella's mouth. "Yeah," she said. "Who knew Brownies would bounce?!"

At the campfire, Mrs. Scott passed out paper bags. "What do we do with these?" Kiara asked. You can't cook bacon in a paper bag!"

"Watch," Mrs. Scott said. She gave each girl four strips of bacon and showed them how to grease the inside of the bag with one piece and then layer the others in the bottom. Then she gave each of them an egg. "Crack it on a rock and drop the egg into the nest of bacon," she said.

Ella plopped her egg onto the bacon. She wiped her slimy hands on her pants and quickly folded the bag to hide its unappetizing contents. "I think I'll have a granola bar for breakfast."

"Be patient," Mrs. Scott said, showing the girls how to use their roasting sticks to hold their bags above the coals. "Camp cooking takes longer, but you can enjoy the nature around you while you cook."

Ella watched the early morning sun straining to break through the low, mousy clouds. In spots, it bounced off the dew and exploded into sparkly patches that looked like crushed diamonds. The crisp morning breeze brushed her face and picked up pieces of her hair to twirl in its chilly fingers. Ella smelled the green freshness of the pine trees that towered around the camp. The odor of the damp earth reminded her of the mushrooms in Mimi's refrigerator.

Finally, Ella closed her eyes and listened. Girls chirped excitedly. Campfire coals hissed and popped. Bacon sizzled in her paper bag— but something wasn't right. As noisy as it was around the campfire, it was also eerily quiet.

Why aren't the birds singing? Ella wondered.

7

CACHE ME IF YOU CAN

After pigging out on bag-cooked eggs and bacon—Kiara like hers so much she cooked a second bag—the girls grabbed their backpacks and listened to Mrs. Scott give instructions for geocaching.

"What's a 'geo'?" Kiara asked. "And how are we gonna catch one?"

"I was wondering the same thing," Ella whispered.

"Really?" Pari whined.

Avery leaned over to Pari. "They don't know any better," she said. "They're only Brownies. They haven't done the geocaching activity yet."

"Your team will be your tent mates," Mrs. Scott said. "One of the Junior Girl Scouts on each team will carry a GPS device."

"I have a cell phone," Avery proudly announced. "I got it for my birthday, and it has GPS. I've even got a hand-cranked charger in case my battery goes dead."

"Perfect," Mrs. Scott said. "Just remember, you can use your cell phone for GPS only. Now, geocaching is like a treasure hunt," she explained. "I'll give each team a set of coordinates. When you find the area, you'll search for the hidden cache."

"Wow!" Kiara said, clapping her hands together rapidly in excitement. "Who knew we'd get cash!"

Mrs. Scott shook her head. "No," she said. "The word sounds like cash, but it's spelled C-A-C-H-E. It's another name for a hiding place, or something found in a hiding place."

Mrs. Scott saw Kiara's disappointment. "Kiara, the real treasure is all the great sights, sounds, and smells you'll discover while looking," she added. "There's also a specific geocaching badge for Junior Girl Scouts to earn."

Mrs. Scott gave GPS coordinates to each team and a whistle to each girl. "Adults will be near at all times. If you need help, blow your whistle."

"I could have used a whistle when I first walked into the camp," Ella muttered, remembering the muddy ordeal of her arrival.

Kiara looked at the counselors and leaders. "Where's your cousin Christina?" she asked Ella.

"She's working with the Daisy Scouts camped nearby. She's coming back to our award ceremony, though." Ella thought of her missing sash and frowned.

"There are important things to remember," Mrs. Scott continued as she passed out garbage bags. "Never disturb any plants or animals and leave things the way you found them."

"What are these bags for?" Ella asked.

"Another meal in a bag?" Kiara suggested.

"Unfortunately, some people throw trash on the ground when they're hiking," Mrs. Scott replied. "While we look for caches, we'll also look for trash. It's a way for geocaching Girl Scouts to help the environment. It's called 'Cache in, Trash out'."

Kiara tucked the trash bag in the neck of her shirt so that it hung behind her like a cape. She blew her whistle and held her hands out like a super hero. "Follow me, girls!" she commanded. "It's time to save the environment!"

But all Kiara and Ella could do was follow Avery and Pari, who walked ahead of them staring selfishly at the phone and chatting nonstop about clothes, and hair, and yes, even boys!

"I wish we had our own GPS," Ella complained. She held out the tail of her shirt like it was a frilly dress, stuck out her pinkies, and walked on her tiptoes pretending to wear high heels. "We could go faster without the fashionistas!"

Kiara giggled. "We'll probably act like that in a few years."

"Let's hope not," Ella said. "The only fashion accessory I'm worried about is my sash!"

"But you have to admit this is a pretty walk," Kiara said.

Ella nodded in agreement. Sunlight frolicked on the dappled path that was padded with freshly-fallen pine straw. Red, yellow, and brown leaves in every shape imaginable formed a colorful carpet beneath their feet. Soft, feathery, ferns grew on either side of the trail. Ella still heard no birds, except a black crow squawking like an old lady with a sore throat.

Ella wondered if anyone else noticed the lack of birds. She feared if she said anything about it, Pari would say that all the birds had migrated south, give some other scientific reason, or call her a stupid baby Brownie. Ella kept the bird thoughts to herself.

Suddenly Avery and Pari stopped. "This is it!" Avery said. "The cache is in this area. And look! There's even a clue to help us locate it!"

"What does it say?" Ella asked, eagerly trying to see the phone.

"I wish I knew," Avery said. She read a long series of random letters:

Vg'f abg va urnira,
vg'f abg ba rnegu,
vg'f n xabg ba n gerr.
Nfx n sevraq gb uryc
lbh frr.

8

KNOT IN A TREE

"Should I blow the whistle?" Kiara asked as her frustrated teammates pored over the nonsensical clue.

"No!" Pari said sternly. "I want to earn my Independence Badge. If I call for help every time I run into a problem, do you think I'll get it?"

"She's right," Avery agreed. "We should figure this out on our own."

"Maybe it's a secret code," Ella suggested.

"It's getting hot," Pari said, taking off her jacket and fanning her face as the sun climbed higher in the sky.

"Actually, I didn't think about a code," Avery said. "I thought it was gobbledygook. Thanks, Ella."

Avery's "thanks" was music to Ella's ears. She asked to see Avery's phone.

Pari fanned her face harder. "Uhhhhh!" she cried. "There are gnats in these woods, I'm hot and sticky, and my hair is frizzing. If you know so much, Miss Smarty Pants, figure it out fast!"

Ella sat on a boulder to concentrate. Her fingers flew across her sister's phone. In just a few minutes, she stood up with a huge smile. "I got it!" she exclaimed. "This is something called ROT13 code. The letters A through M are stacked above the letters N through Z and you substitute the letter you want to use with the one above or below it. Give me a pencil and paper, quick!"

Pari dug a pink notebook out of her backpack. "Here," she said.

"I've got a pencil," Kiara added.

Ella wrote the code key and together the girls solved the puzzle.

"OK," Avery said. "Here's what the clue says: It's not in heaven, it's not on earth, it's a knot in a tree. Ask a friend to help you see."

"That didn't help," Pari said. "I still don't know what we're looking for."

"Me neither," Kiara said. "How do you tie a knot in a tree?"

"You've got it all wrong," Avery explained. From their many nature walks with Papa, she and Ella knew about tree knots. "A tree knot is a shallow hole in a tree—the perfect place to hide something!"

"That's it!" Ella agreed, shaking her sister's hand ceremoniously. "It's not in the sky and it's not on the ground, so what we're looking for is in a tree!"

"Nice work, ladies!" Kiara shouted, applauding them with her usual excited clapping.

"Let's split up so we can find it," Avery suggested.

Avery and Pari looked on the left side of the path, while Ella and Kiara looked on the right. It wasn't long before Kiara yelled, "I found one!"

"Really!?" Avery yelled, leaping over a small bush and trotting across the path with Pari close on her heels.

"Yeah!" Kiara said, opening up her plastic trash bag. "My first piece of trash! It looks like someone likes potato chips. I love 'em too. I wish this bag wasn't empty."

"You've got to be kidding me," Pari whined.

"Finding trash is another important reason we're here," Ella snapped. "You are so negative!"

"Maybe she's on to something," Avery said, eyeing the surrounding trees. "If there's a chip bag, someone had to drop it, and maybe that someone was the person who hid the cache, or at least the last person who found it."

"But geocachers aren't supposed to leave trash," Ella said. "It's against the rules."

"Maybe they dropped it by accident," Avery said, surveying the area until her eyes landed on a knot in a nearby tree. "Hey, look! That one's big enough to hold a cache."

"And it looks like an upside down heart," Pari said. "That's my favorite shape."

The girls waded through the brush to the tree. "I'm the tallest," Pari said. "I can reach it." She stood on her tiptoes and walked her sparkly nails up the tree bark. "Can't do it," she admitted, letting out an exasperated breath. "Guess I should've worn high heels instead of sneakers."

"Kiara and I can reach it," Ella said, climbing onto her friend's shoulders. But no matter how hard she strained, Ella couldn't reach the cache either. "Your time's up, friend," Kiara said, struggling to balance Ella on her shoulders."

"Our only option is to work together," Avery said. "Let's make a human pyramid."

"You mean a Girl Scout human pyramid," Kiara said.

Avery got on her hands and knees. "You're next, Pari," she said. Pari moved down to her hands and knees next to Avery. Kiara climbed onto the two girls' backs. "Hurry, Ella!" Avery urged as her face grew as hot and red as her favorite salsa.

Ella looked skeptically at the tower. She trusted Kiara, and she sort of trusted her sister, but she wondered, "Can I trust Pari?" Summoning her courage, she climbed the pyramid of girls like a crafty cat. On top, she easily reached inside the knot. Her fingers felt a small metal box about the size of a match box. But as soon as she gripped the box, a deep, gruff voice bellowed, "Hey! What are you doing!? Get away from there!"

9

ROAMING WITCH

Startled by the voice, Ella lost her balance and the pyramid of girls crumbled beneath her. The tree bark scraped her forehead as she went down, down, and down until she hit the ground in a tangle of arms and legs. As the other girls worked to stand, Ella looked up and saw a man staring down at her.

"Are you OK?" he asked.

"Ahhh," Ella answered, not quite sure.

"What are you girls doing in the woods alone?" he asked. "Don't you know it's not safe to do that?"

"What are you doing here?" Avery answered him with another question. She knew that none of the camp counselors were men, and she knew she shouldn't talk to strangers. She placed her hand on her whistle, ready to put it to her mouth at a moment's notice.

The man glanced at the trash bags tied to the girls' belts. "Probably the same thing you are," he said. "My partner and I are maintaining the trails."

"So you work at Camp Poplar?" Pari asked.

The man nodded. "You could say that," he answered.

"Where's your partner?" Ella asked.

"He's with the truck on another trail," he answered. Spotting Ella's Brownie pin he said, "You must be Girl Scouts!"

"We are!" Kiara said proudly.

The man, unusually tall with bright blue eyes, leaned forward as if to tell them a secret. "You girls really shouldn't be in these woods," he warned. "There's a crazy old woman who lives by Cryptic Lake. She's been seen roaming this area. Some people say she's a witch! If you see her, run away as fast as you can. From what I hear, she can turn people into other creatures—lizards and such!"

The girls' eyes grew wide. They looked at each other and shuddered. They were all thinking the same thing. *Was the legendary lizard, Tic-Lic, really a human—maybe a Girl Scout who got lost in the woods?*

10

WATCH OUT!

"Did you find..." the man began when a shrill whistle made them all jump.

"Girls!" Mrs. Scott yelled. "Time for lunch!"

"I better go," the man said, quickly disappearing through the undergrowth.

The campfire was cold when the girls returned to camp. "Awwww," Kiara whined, looking at the ashes. "How are we gonna roast hot dogs with no fire?"

"Come and get it!" Mrs. Scott said, again banging on her pot. Loaves of bread, jars of peanut butter and jelly, lunchmeat, and cheese filled a long table. Beads of condensation dripped down the sides of big glass jugs of lemonade perched at the end.

"I hope all of you found your cache and a lot of trash," Mrs. Scott said. Then, she held up a cookie cutter in the shape of a trefoil, the Girl Scout symbol. "As you know, 'trefoil' means three leaves," she explained. "Each leaf stands for a part of the Girl Scout Promise. Before we make our trefoil-shaped sandwiches, I'd like each of you to make the Girl Scout Sign and recite the Girl Scout Promise."

The girls raised three fingers on their right hands, held down their pinky fingers with their thumbs, and recited: "*On my honor, I will try:* To serve God and my country, To help people at all times, and to live by the Girl Scout Law."

"Very good," Mrs. Scott said. "Now, extend the left hand of friendship to the person on your right."

Ella was suddenly reminded of her trip with Mimi to the Wayne Gordon House in Savannah, Georgia, where Girl Scout founder Juliette Gordon Low was born. The house, completed in 1821, had just been renovated. It was so beautiful that Ella could imagine

"Daisy" (as Juliette was known as a little girl) running through the grand rooms.

There, Ella had learned a lot of Girl Scout history including the story of the left hand of friendship. Juliette Gordon Low became friends with a man in England named Lord Baden-Powell, who had started a group called the Girl Guides. Juliette brought the idea back to the U.S. in 1910 and formed the Girl Scouts.

Lord Baden-Powell chose a left-handed shake for the Girl Guides, and Juliette kept it for the Girl Scouts. It is believed that he got the idea from a legend about two tribal groups in West Africa that never got along. The warriors carried shields on their left arms to protect themselves from their enemies. When they decided to stop fighting, they threw down their shields and greeted each other with the left hand of peace and friendship.

Ella turned to her left, expecting to grab Kiara's hand. Instead, she was looking straight at Pari. Ella wasn't sure she was ready to throw down her shield until Pari gave her back her sash.

Reluctantly, Ella held out her hand. At first, Pari hesitated. Mrs. Scott, who was waiting until everyone was holding hands, looked at them impatiently. Finally, Pari grabbed Ella's hand. "Ouch!" Ella complained. "Watch those fake fingernails. They scratch!"

"Now," Mrs. Scott said, "I want you to look at the person whose hand you're holding and recite the Girl Scout Law."

Ella took a deep breath and blew it out slowly. Together the girls recited: "*I will do my best* to be honest and fair, friendly and helpful, considerate and caring, courageous and strong, and responsible for what I say and do, *and* to respect myself and others, respect authority, use resources wisely, make the world a better place, and be a sister to every Girl Scout."

The words of the Girl Scout Law stung Ella like a nagging bumblebee. *Have I really been obeying the Girl Scout Law?* she asked herself, already knowing the answer. *But how can I be a Girl Scout sister to someone who's not telling the truth?*

Avery interrupted her thoughts. "When you get your sandwich, let's meet in our tent," Avery whispered. "We should talk about the cache."

Ella and Kiara were first in line. "Hurry!" Ella whispered, slapping together turkey, cheese, and bread and pressing the trefoil cookie cutter into it. "I think I know where my sash is!" As soon as they finished making their sandwiches, the girls grabbed their lemonade and hurried to the tent to get there before Avery and Pari did.

"Watch the door," Ella told Kiara. She crawled to Pari's side of the tent. "She doesn't think I'm interested in girlie things like nail polish," Ella said. "So this nail case is the perfect hiding spot."

Ella scratched around in the case, nervously glancing over her shoulder.

"Find anything?" Kiara asked.

"Nothing but her stupid nail polish," Ella said, disappointed.

When Avery and Pari got to the tent, the girls sat on the tent floor criss-cross applesauce to eat their trefoil sandwiches. Kiara had a stack of them. "I guess three leaves aren't enough for me," she said with a giggle. "I made enough for a whole Girl Scout tree!"

But Avery had more on her mind than lunch. "Mrs. Scott said we're going canoeing on the lake this afternoon," she began. "But I'm curious about what was in that cache. It sure seemed like that man was curious, too."

"There's only one way to find out," Ella said. She thrust her right hand deep into her jeans pocket.

"Do you think we should go back to the tree?" Avery asked.

"Don't have to," Ella replied, pulling the small metal box from her pocket. "I've got the box right here."

"Hey!" Pari exclaimed. "Why didn't you tell us?"

Remembering the Girl Scout Law she had just recited, Ella bit her tongue before replying with a smart remark. "I haven't had a chance," she said. "Mrs. Scott walked back to camp with us, and I didn't want her to know I'd taken the cache. I didn't mean to. I had my hand around it when I fell."

"That's OK," Avery said. "We'll get it back somehow. But now, let's see what's inside!"

Ella tugged on the little latch. The lid creaked furiously as she pulled it back, as if it didn't want them to know the secrets it held. Ella turned the cache over and dumped its contents. There were several trinkets—a green plastic four-leaf clover, a string bracelet, a 1962 penny, and a tiny yellow troll doll with pink hair and green eyes. There was also a miniature logbook, with the dates and names of those who had found the cache before.

"Is that all that's in there?" Avery asked, running her finger around the inside of the box. "Wait! I feel something. Pari, hand me a nail file."

Avery ran the file inside the edge of the box and a tiny orange scroll fell to the floor. Carefully she unrolled it and read to the girls:

CANOE CONUNDRUM

Ella counted Avery, Kiara, Pari, and then herself. "There are four of us," she said. "Is someone warning us to watch out?"

"Watch out for what?" Kiara asked.

"Maybe the roaming witch the man at the tree told us about?" Ella said.

"You're being silly," Pari said. "I'm not buying into those campfire ghost stories. Besides, why would we be roaming the woods at 10 p.m.? There's no way Mrs. Scott would allow that. If I'm not already cuddled up in my sleeping bag at 10 p.m., I'll either be giving myself a pedicure or rolling my hair. I want to look good when I add badges to my sash at the award ceremony."

Ella looked squarely at Pari. "I'll have my sash by then too," she remarked with confidence.

Avery picked up the trinkets and started dropping them in the metal container. PLINK! PLINK! PLINK! The noise got her thinking. "Pari," she said, "didn't you say that lady you saw outside the campfire circle last night was carrying a metal box?"

"Yes," Pari answered. "I heard it clank when she bumped a tree with it. But it was much bigger than this one."

"Brownies! Juniors!" Mrs. Scott called. "Lunch is over! It's time for our afternoon activities."

Ella pushed wisps of blond hair off her face. "The only activity I want to do," she announced, "is find the meaning of the scroll."

Avery looked closely at her sister. "What's that on your forehead?" she asked. "It can't be Mimi's lipstick this time!"

Ella brushed her fingers lightly across a rough, sore spot. "I guess I scraped my head on the tree when I was trying to reach the cache," she said. "It's not that noticeable, is it?"

"Not if you don't mind looking like a big, scary Cyclops," Pari said. "But I've got something that will take care of that." She grabbed a paisley quilted bag stuffed with beauty products. "Hold still," she ordered Ella.

"What are you doing?" Ella asked. "Is that makeup? You know I'm too young to wear makeup."

"Just enough to cover that mark," Pari said, her hands moving with swift efficiency. "I'm too young to wear makeup, too, but I get to play with it as long as I'm not leaving home. Just close your eyes and I'll be done in a second."

"Ahhh, Pari," Avery said, trying to get her attention.

"Almost done," Pari said as she grabbed a fluffy brush. "Let me add a little blush and... there! No more ugly forehead mark."

"Didn't you forget something?" Kiara said.

Pari winked. "I think she looks much, much better!"

"GIRLS!" Mrs. Scott called again. "Let's go—NOW!"

Avery shrugged. "Guess we better go!"

Hiking to the lake, Kiara giggled every time she looked at Ella. "What is wrong with you?" Ella asked.

"It's just that...just that..."she said, before giggling again.

"I wish you'd stop being so silly," Ella said. "We have two mysteries on our hands and we need to be on the lookout for clues."

Eventually, the trail ducked out of the woods and wound up a hill. When the girls reached the top, they waded through a patch of tall grass before catching sight of the lake, sparkling in the sunlight and smooth as a mirror.

"Wow!" Ella exclaimed. "Cryptic Lake!"

"It doesn't look too scary," Kiara said, "as long as Tic-Lic takes a long afternoon nap!"

"No, it doesn't look scary at all," Ella agreed. "It's quite beautiful, actually." She pointed at a group of canoes bobbing near the shore. "And it looks like our next activity is ready and waiting for us."

At the lake, Mrs. Scott gave a long speech on water safety and demonstrated the proper way to row a canoe before passing out bright orange life jackets to each girl.

"It's your turn to navigate the course," Mrs. Scott instructed. "Christina will ride with you as your camp counselor. Avery, since only four girls can ride in a canoe, you'll stay here with me as my safety helper. You all need to follow the string of buoys and work together. Teams that don't work together usually end up going in a circle. If you need help, use your whistle. Oh, and girls," she added, "this isn't a race, but the first team to reach the finish line has no evening kapers tonight!"

"Can't we switch teams?" Pari begged Mrs. Scott.

"No," she replied.

"Looks like I'm stuck with the baby Brownies," Pari mumbled.

When Mrs. Scott gave the signal, the girls hurried to their canoes.

"I'm glad we got the green one!" Kiara said, clapping her hands nervously.

"Who's gonna push it into the water?" Pari asked. "I don't want to get my new shoes wet and filthy!"

"You're at camp, not a fashion show!" Ella growled.

Christina quickly took over. "Ella and Pari, you climb aboard. Kiara and I will push the canoe into the water." As she took hold of the canoe, Christina peered at Ella's face. "Hey, Ella," she began, but was quickly interrupted by Mrs. Scott's shrill whistle. "Time to get started, everyone!" she called.

The girls pushed mightily, their feet sliding in the slimy green mud, until the canoe slipped into the water and floated freely. Christina slipped into the canoe while Pari and Ella grabbed Kiara's life jacket to help her climb in. The girls pulled and pulled until she finally landed head first into the canoe. Her feet, sticking straight up into the air, kicked wildly as the canoe rocked like a baby's cradle.

"Where's your shoe?" Ella asked, noticing her friend's bare foot.

"Oh, no!" Kiara exclaimed. "It must be stuck in the mud!"

Ella leaned over the canoe's side to look for the shoe. For the first time, she saw what Kiara had been giggling about. Her face had changed color! No longer white, it was a rich shade of coffee brown.

She glared at Pari who shrugged innocently. "Sorry! The only makeup I have matches my skin, not yours, unfortunately."

Ella grabbed a handful of water to wash her face and as she did, Kiara's lime green shoe popped up from the bottom. "Here," she said, handing the shoe to Kiara, but letting the murky water inside it spill out onto Pari's pristine sneakers.

"Heyyyyyy!" Pari cried. "Watch what you're doing!"

Ella shrugged as innocently as Pari had and said, "So sorry! I had no idea there was so much water in Kiara's shoe."

When Pari's anger had cooled off, she and Kiara began rowing as Mrs. Scott had shown them. But it was too late. The other canoes quickly passed them.

"We're losing!" Ella yelled. "Let me row!"

She swapped places with Kiara and began to row faster, but Pari didn't. "We're starting to go in a circle!" Ella grumbled.

"It's your fault!" Pari shouted.

"Stop rowing!" Christina ordered. "Every time I slap the side of the canoe, row. You have to work together."

Soon the canoe corrected course and aimed for the finish line. They passed one canoe and then another.

"We're pulling ahead!" Ella exclaimed.

"But wh-wh-what is that f-f-following us?!" Kiara asked as she stared in terror at the canoe's wake.

FREAKY FROG LEGS

"It must be Tic-Lic!" Kiara screamed as she saw the glint of sunlight on glistening scales. She stood up, growing more anxious by the second.

"Kiara, sit down!" Christina commanded. "You're going to—"

It was too late. The canoe rocked violently side to side until...KERSPLASH! It flipped over, dumping the girls into the icy-cold lake water.

The girls gasped for air as they bobbed on the surface like four floating corks. "What just happened?" Pari sputtered.

"Everyone stay calm," Christina urged the girls. "Help is on the way. And we're all wearing life jackets, so we're OK." She waved her arm at the oncoming rescue boat.

"There it is!" Kiara screamed, reaching for her whistle. But when she blew, all that came out was a bubble of murky green lake water. "Help!" she cried. "He's gonna get me!"

Ella grabbed a floating oar and poked at the scaly beast headed straight for them.

"Ella, don't!" Avery warned.

Poked by the oar, a long, black water snake popped his head up out of the water, startled by the interruption of his journey. He stared at them with beady black eyes and then continued on his way around the capsized canoe.

A team of camp counselors pulled beside the girls, helped them aboard, and threw blankets around each girl. When they reached the shore, the last of the canoes had landed. One team of girls was already doing a victory dance.

Kiara hung her head. "I'm really sorry about that," she apologized to her teammates.

"It's OK, Kiara," Ella said. "If I had seen that snake following us, I would've thought it was Tic-Lic too."

Pari parted the hair that was plastered to her face and peered at Kiara. Ella braced herself for the tongue-lashing she knew her friend was about to get. But instead of chastising Kiara as Ella expected, Pari burst into laughter.

"I wonder if there's a Girl Scout badge for falling in the lake and surviving," Pari said. "That was scary, but kind of fun!"

Ella twisted her shirt, squeezing a shower of lake water onto the ground. "Or a special waterproof b-b-badge!" she chimed in through chattering teeth.

Christina smiled at the waterlogged crew. "That's the spirit," she said. "You just gotta laugh sometimes!"

"Let's get you girls warm and dry," Mrs. Scott said. "I'm glad we already have a nice warm fire going."

She led the shivering girls to the fire and parked them beside it. "Sit here until you're dry," she said.

"Hey, you guys!" Avery said as she joined the group. "You might have won if you hadn't capsized," she said. "I was cheering for you from the shore!"

"It was my fault, Avery," Kiara said. "I was afraid that Tic-Lic was following us, and that's why I stood up in the canoe." She looked over at Pari and Ella. "Thanks for not getting mad at me," Kiara told her teammates. "I let my imagination get the best of me."

"Don't worry, Kiara," Christina said. "We are all Girl Scout sisters, and sisters help each other and forgive each other. You guys were working together as a real team! You should be proud of that."

"It did feel good when we were skimming across that water like a dragonfly, didn't it?" Pari asked Ella.

Ella, sitting with her elbows propped on her knees and chin cupped in her hands, stared into the fire. "Yes it did," she said. Then she looked at Pari. "But if a sister took something from someone, even as a joke, she'd give it back."

Pari took a deep breath and looked straight at Ella. "Ella, I know I haven't been very nice to you," she said. "Since moving to America, I've missed my mom and grandmother terribly. My dad's great, but he's not so good at girl talk. When I became friends with Avery, I wanted her to be the sister I didn't have. I was jealous of you. Now, I'm realizing I could have three sisters! You and Kiara could certainly use another big sister to teach you all the things you need to know."

"Does that mean you're giving me back my sash?" Ella asked.

"If I had it, I would!" Pari said. "But I'm telling you, I DON'T have it."

CROAK! CROAK!

Kiara stood up straight and whirled around to look for the source of the loud noise. "Does anyone know what sound Tic-Lic makes?" she asked with a shaky voice.

Ella said, "No worries, Kiara. That's just a frog."

"Oh, really? A frog?" Pari asked, her face breaking into a big smile. "You might as well catch it, Ella. Remember when you lost the sleeping bag race? We said the loser had to catch a frog. A bet's a bet, you know."

"I'll be glad to catch it," Ella announced. "And when I do, I'll come and put it right in your lap!"

"You better not," Pari warned.

Ella rose from her seat and crept slowly toward the sound. Although her clothes were almost dry, her soggy shoes squelched with every step. She saw a bush quiver and heard something plop onto the dirt. Finally, she spotted the slimy green frog. But every time she took a step, it hopped several times to stay ahead of her.

Ella loosened her shoelaces and stepped out of her noisy shoes. When she did, she noticed a piece of trash on the ground. "Doing my good turn," she mumbled, stuffing the paper in her pocket.

Ella tiptoed toward the frog, then lunged for it, making a dome with her hands to trap it on the ground. She scooped up the frog, tucked him into one of her shoes, and covered the opening with her hand. As she marched triumphantly back to the fire, something in the distance caught Ella's eye. As the shape got closer, she could tell it was an old, gray-hair-in-a-bun woman, walking with her eyes fixed on the ground. She was poking at something with a long stick. When she took a step, Ella could hear the sound of clanking metal.

Ella ran back to join the other girls. "I saw her!" she cried, breathless when she reached the fire.

"So the frog's a girl?" Kiara said.

"No, no," Ella said. "I think it's the woman Pari saw near our campfire last night. I couldn't see her feet, so I don't know if she was wearing muddy boots, but I think she had a metal box. I could hear metal clanking."

She whirled to look at Pari. "I'm sorry I didn't believe you, Pari."

"Could this woman be the roaming witch?" Avery asked.

"Maybe," Ella said. "She looked like she was roaming to me."

Pari shuddered. "I can't believe I was actually talking to a witch!" she said.

Ella, who had forgotten about the frog in her shoe, set her shoe on the ground. FLOP! The frog lurched out beside the fire and hopped towards Pari.

"Ewwwww!" she screamed. "Keep that thing away from me!"

Ella picked up the frog and pointed it at Pari. "Want a slimy kiss?" she asked. "It just might be the prince you've been dreaming of!"

"Please, don't!" Pari said, backing up. "I promise I won't play any more pranks on you!"

Ella could feel the frog's heart pounding against her hand. "I wouldn't be that mean to a poor little froggie," she said. "He clearly doesn't want to be your boyfriend."

Ella gently placed the frog on the ground and noticed something astonishing.

"Look!" she cried. "This frog has five legs!"

KEEP AWAY FROM CRYPTIC LAKE

On the way back to camp, Ella noticed that the lake's mood was changing. Choppy little waves rolled to the shore in steady rhythm. And the famous fog was rising like steam from a pot and floating around the girls' ankles.

The Girl Scouts marched beside several dead trees near the water's edge. Gray Spanish moss hung like old men's beards, wagging in the shy breeze. At the base of the trees, Ella noticed several small dead turtles. *I wonder what happened to them,* she thought.

A few dark clouds began to gather in the sky. Ella wondered if the clouds were headed to a meeting to decide if they should ruin the rest of her camping trip now or postpone their thunderous party for later. She also wondered if the mysterious, roaming witch was conjuring some weather spell that would trap them here—trap them so she could change them into some creepy creature, like the five-legged frog.

When they got to the top of the hill, Kiara turned around for one last look at the lake below. "Is that a fire?" she asked, watching a plume of gray smoke rising from the forest surrounding the lake.

"I don't think that's smoke," Avery said. "It's mist rising from the forest floor. Papa always says that means the rabbits are cooking supper."

Or maybe a witch cooking supper, Ella thought.

When the Girl Scouts reached camp, most of them got busy with their evening kapers. But before Avery, Pari, Ella, and Kiara began their jobs, they changed out of their dirty lake clothes. As Ella changed her pants she heard a crinkly noise in her pocket. She reached in and pulled out the piece of trash she'd picked up while chasing the frog. She started to throw it in the trash bag in the corner of the tent, but something told her to look at it first. She smoothed the rumpled, lined paper on her knee. To her surprise, something was written on it!

"Look at this!" she exclaimed to her tent mates. She read the note:

Keep away from Cryptic Lake or you'll be the next thing that's missing!

14

UP IN SMOKE

Puzzled by their latest clue, the girls tackled the worst of kapers—cleaning the latrine. Inside the building, they checked under every stall to make sure no one else was there. They pulled on rubber gloves and discussed all they knew so far as they cleaned.

First, Ella's sash was still missing. Next, someone was supposed to "watch out" at 10 p.m., according to the scroll hidden in the cache. And then, there was the strange lady who might be the roaming witch, a freaky, five-legged frog, and now a threat that someone might go missing.

"Are we the ones who should stay away from Cryptic Lake?" Kiara asked. "That's OK with me anyway. There's something awfully creepy about that place."

Ella sighed. "I'm not even sure any of those things have anything to do with each other or with my missing sash," she said. "Unless the witch took my sash."

Pari smiled. "At least you have another possible suspect besides me!" she said. "But why would a witch want your sash?"

Avery was happy that Pari and Ella finally seemed to be getting along. But she was unhappy with what she was thinking. "To lure four curious girls into a trap?" she suggested.

"Aaaaaachoooo!" Kiara sneezed after sprinkling cleaner in a sink.

"Did you hear that?" Ella asked.

"How could we not hear that?" Avery asked.

"Not the sneeze," Ella said. "That low, rumbling sound. Listen!"

"Maybe it's thunder," Kiara suggested.

"It sounds like a big truck," Avery said. "But why would a big truck be near the camp at night?"

"Seems suspicious," Ella said. "But right now, everything seems suspicious."

When the girls finished cleaning the latrine, they walked back to the campfire for the lighting ceremony. Mrs. Scott handed each of them a stick, and a marker. "Write a wish on the stick and when it burns, your wishes will rise into the air to come true!"

Avery, Pari, Ella, and Kiara leaned their wish sticks on the teepee of wood, as four Girl Scouts holding candles stood outside the fire ring at the four compass points. One by one, the girls brought their candles to light one corner of the fire and speak their lines:

"I am the North Wind. I bring the cold that builds endurance."

"I am the South Wind. I bring the warmth of friendship."

"I am the East Wind. I bring the light of day."

"I am the West Wind. I bring the night sky, the moon, and stars."

Next, the girls assembled hobo dinners—foil packets filled with a hamburger patty, potatoes, onion, and carrots—and placed them on the hot coals around the fire.

As their suppers cooked, Mrs. Scott asked each team to perform an impromptu skit or song. Ella, Avery, Pari, and Kiara sang a patriotic American song.

Ella was surprised when Pari linked arms with her and Kiara and they all swayed in time with the music. "Sing with us!" Kiara urged all the Girl Scouts around the campfire as they sang the chorus over and over.

It was a beautiful scene, and Ella was happy that four very different girls had become true "Girl Scouts together." She spotted her wish stick, the black words written on it slowly turning into smoke rising to the heavens. Her mind turned back to her missing sash. "I wish I could find my sash and solve this mystery," she whispered.

15

SISTERS UNDER THE STARS

After supper, Mrs. Scott and Mrs. Dunn led the girls to a nearby clearing for stargazing. With their legs shuffling along together in a line, they resembled a centipede snaking along with flashlight eyes.

In the clearing, the girls spread blankets and lay on their backs, pointing out every constellation they could spot.

"What is that?" Kiara asked, amazed as a streak of bright light flashed across the sky and seemed to drop into the forest.

"It's a shooting star!" Avery answered.

"Amazing!" Kiara said, clapping. "That's the first one I've ever seen. I wonder if we could find it?"

Ella knew the answer to Kiara's question. She knew that Avery and Pari knew the answer, too. But she waited to see what they would say. Pari certainly had seemed to change, but this would be another chance to prove it.

"I truly wish we could find it," Pari said. "That would be super cool. But it's really not a star at all. A shooting star is just pieces of rock or dust left behind by a comet. Most of them burn up on the way down. Unless they're big, there's nothing to find."

A Girl Scout, overhearing their conversation, softly began singing another favorite Girl Scout song called Shooting Star. A camp counselor gently strummed her guitar as the girls joined in:

"Please won't you catch a shooting star for me
And take it with you on your way.

Although we just met, you're the one I won't forget.

Hope some kind of wind blows you back my way.

98

Chorus:

And I was thinking maybe somewhere down the road,
After all our stories have been told,
I'll sit and think of you, the good friend I once knew,
Shot through my life like a shooting star."

Ella smiled. Pari had answered with kindness. And she knew that she'd never forget this, her first successful camping trip, and the feeling of having not just her sister and best friend experience it with her, but an entire sisterhood of Girl Scouts.

"OK, girls," Mrs. Scott said finally. "Guess we better head back for lights out. Our last full day at camp tomorrow is a busy one. I saw a few dark clouds earlier, so I hope we're not in for a shower tonight!"

All the girls groaned, reluctant to leave the star show above them and the feeling of camaraderie.

On the way back, Ella's flashlight highlighted ridges on the path. "Are those tire tracks?" she asked Avery.

"Looks like it to me," Avery said.

"Hmmm," Ella mused. "Do you think that truck we heard when we were cleaning the latrine made these?"

"Probably," Avery said.

Kiara tapped Ella's arm. "Look!" she said, pointing into the woods beside the path.

A swaying light glowed slowly through the trees.

"Do you think that's our falling star?" Kiara asked.

"No way," Ella answered, her eyes growing wide. "It looks like someone carrying a lantern."

"Could it be a Girl Scout or a counselor?" Kiara asked.

"I don't think so," Ella answered. "What time is it?"

Avery looked at her phone. "It's 9:55," she answered.

"Almost 10 p.m.!" Ella cried. "That's when the note said that someone should watch out. Maybe the light in the woods is the roaming witch! She's looking for us!"

The girls walked faster and faster until their walk became a jog. Suddenly, Kiara hit the brakes. Pari smacked into Kiara, knocking her face first onto the path. Another Girl Scout ran into Pari, knocking her on top of Kiara. One after another, Girl Scouts went down like tumbling dominoes.

Ella and Avery helped pull Pari and Kiara to their feet. "Owww," grumbled Kiara, brushing leaves and pine needles from her bright pink T-shirt.

"Why did you stop?" Pari asked Kiara.

"I saw a piece of trash," Kiara said, "and I wanted to pick it up."

Ella could see Pari trying hard not to lose her temper. Even she was a little annoyed with her friend—until Kiara showed her the piece of trash. It was another potato chip bag, exactly like the one they'd found under the tree!

16

SCRATCHING SHADOW

"Maybe the warning wasn't for us after all," Avery said, when they'd made it safely back to their tent.

"Maybe not," Ella said. "But something strange was going on in this camp tonight. There are too many coincidences."

"What if," Avery began, "the man at the tree has something to do with all this. He was awfully interested in what we were doing."

"That's right," Kiara agreed. "Maybe he's the one who likes potato chips so much, or maybe the witch likes to snack on them while she brews disgusting potions in her black cauldron."

"I don't know," Ella said. "If that man is involved with whatever's going on, then where does our roaming witch fit in?"

Avery pretended to pull out her hair in frustration. "Ahhhhh!" she grumbled. "It's all so confusing. Anyway, we should get the cache back in the tree on our way to the ropes course tomorrow."

"Good idea," Ella said. "Maybe we can find another clue there."

Pari yawned. "I'm pooped," she said. "Can we work on this tomorrow? I want to get up early so I can fix everyone's hair. Since it's our last full day of camp, I want to get some cute pictures of all of us."

"No makeup, right?" Ella asked.

"No makeup," Pari said. "I promise."

"No spiders?" Kiara asked.

"Well, I don't know about that," Avery said, grinning.

Avery and Pari climbed into their sleeping bags. But before Ella and Kiara did the same, they checked their sleeping bags thoroughly, even turning them inside out.

Avery giggled and told Pari, "Ha! They don't trust us."

"You better watch out," Ella said. "Kiara and I might just have a few pranks of our own."

"You wouldn't dare," Avery said.

"Sleep tight, sister!" Ella said in a super-sweet voice.

"And sleep tight, Tic-Lic!" Kiara added, zipping her sleeping bag and kissing the zipper pull.

Soon, Ella could hear the soft snores of her tent mates. But she flopped and she flipped, she tossed and she turned. Giving up on sleep, she quietly unzipped her sleeping bag and crawled to her water bottle. She popped the top open and took a drink.

Just when she did, a jagged scar of lightning ripped across the sky and threw a shadow on the side of the tent. Something was outside! Ella could make out a long nose and long, sharp nails scratching on the tent fabric.

BOOM! A thunderous crash echoed through the sky. Ella not only heard it, she felt the vibration in her chest. The noise made her jump so high she hit her head on the tent roof. She lunged for Kiara in the closest sleeping bag and shook her friend awake.

"Kiara! Kiara! Wake up!" Ella pleaded. "She's out there!"

Kiara muttered something, wiped her face with her hand, and turned over. "Kiara!" Ella insisted. "It's her! The roaming witch!"

17

ONE GOOD PRANK DESERVES ANOTHER

When Kiara heard "witch" she bolted upright. "Are you sure?"

"Y-y-yess, I am sh-sh-sure," Ella said. She pointed to where she had seen the scratching shadow.

"I don't see anything," Kiara said, hugging her trembling friend. "Maybe it was just a tree limb or Mrs. Scott making sure our light was out. Do you think we should wake Avery and Pari?"

"Not yet," Ella said, her heart gradually slowing to a normal beat. "Maybe it was my silly imagination. It probably was Mrs. Scott checking on us. But I don't think I can go to sleep for a while."

"Since I'm awake now too, we might as well do something to pass the time. How about some pranks?" Kiara suggested, her eyes sparkling with mischief.

The girls quickly made a plan.. As the sprinkles of rain bouncing on their tent turned into a downpour, they set to work, quiet as Brownie elves. Occasionally a boom of thunder caused them to jump, but they'd giggle nervously and keep working.

Avery and Pari never seemed to notice the noisy storm. When they had completed their dastardly plan, Ella and Kiara climbed back into their sleeping bags and dozed off to sleep.

ZIP!! Ella awakened to the sound of someone unzipping the tent flap. At first she gasped, but realizing it was daylight, turned to see Mrs. Scott standing in the doorway. She looked tired. "Sorry, it's too wet for a fire this morning, girls," she said, tossing in a handful of granola bars. "This will have to do until lunch time."

"Mrs. Scott," Ella asked, "did you come to our tent last night?"

"No, Ella, I didn't," she said, yawning. "Several of us adults were up all night checking the weather on my phone. I was afraid I might have to move all you girls into the latrine to sleep."

Kiara wrinkled her nose. "I'm sure glad we didn't have to do that!" she said.

Mrs. Scott nodded and smiled. "Yes, thank goodness we didn't have to do that. As soon as you eat, get dressed and meet in the campfire circle. It's rope course day!"

Avery reached for her sleeping bag zipper and tugged. Nothing happened. She tugged again. Still nothing. "Hey!" she said. "My zipper's stuck!"

"I'll help you," Pari said, tugging at her own zipper. "Wait! Mine's stuck too!"

Ella and Kiara covered their mouths to trap their giggles.

"What did you do?" Avery asked the two accusingly.

"My grandmother packed some super glue in my bag," Kiara said. "She said it might come in handy, and it did!"

"You glued our zippers?" Avery asked.

"One good prank deserves another," Ella said with a grin.

"I guess I can eat all the granola bars I want, since you two can't get out of your sleeping bags," Kiara said, peeling back the paper on her first one.

"Oh, no you can't!" Pari said, wriggling out of her sleeping bag like a butterfly coming out of a chrysalis. "There's more than one way to get out of a sleeping bag!"

When the girls finished their breakfast, Pari braided Avery's hair into two pigtails that hung down her back while Kiara and Ella dressed. "That looks good!" Ella admitted.

"I'm glad you like it," Pari said. "because you're next!"

In a jiffy, Pari created a single braid down Ella's back. "That'll keep that wild hair out of your eyes!" she said.

Next, Pari gathered Kiara's hair into a ponytail and tied it with a hot pink bow. Kiara admired her new look in a mirror and nodded approvingly. "You're good at this," she said.

The chatter of girls was rising louder and louder from the campfire circle. Pari and Avery grabbed their socks and shoes. But when Avery pulled on her yellow sock, her foot slid right out the end.

Ella and Kiara howled with laughter again at the shocked look on Avery's face. They doubled over with giggles when Pari discovered the toes were cut out of her neon green socks as well.

Avery glared at her sister. "It's a good thing we brought extras."

"I've got an idea," Pari said, rolling each of the four sock tops into a circle, and then stretching them. "We can each have a headband. It'll help us keep track of each other."

Ella hoped the bright headbands wouldn't help the roaming witch keep track of them as well!

18

POTATO SOUP FOG

"Why did Mrs. Scott call this pea soup fog?" Ella asked as they walked to the rope course area. "It's not green like peas. It's more like potato soup."

"Call it potato soup fog if you like," Avery said. "I just hope it goes away soon."

"These headbands were a great idea," Kiara told Pari. "This stuff is so thick I'm not sure I could see you guys if you weren't wearing them."

"Did you remember the cache?" Avery asked Ella.

Ella tapped her pocket. "Got it!"

The fog made it hard for the girls to tell where they were on the trail, but Avery still had the coordinates in her phone from the last time. When they were near the spot, she motioned for Ella, Kiara, and Pari to fall to the back of the line. She whispered, "No dawdling. Get to the tree, make the pyramid, put the cache back, and catch back up to the line."

The girls left the trail. When they got close enough to see the familiar upside-down, heart-shaped tree knot through the thick fog, they performed their plan like a well-rehearsed circus act. But before Ella placed the metal box back into the tree knot, she followed a hunch. She felt inside the hole to see if anything else had been placed inside. Her hunch was right! She stuffed the note she found in her pocket and slid off the pyramid of friends. "Let's go," she whispered.

At the ropes course, the white ropes blended into the fog. "This is awful," Mrs. Scott said. "Maybe we should call off the rope activities today."

With one voice the girls all groaned, "Nooooooo!" Other whining protests followed.

"It's the funnest thing at camp!" "Now I'll never get to do it!" "I'm sure the fog will clear any minute!" "Pleeeeaaaasssseeee, Mrs Scott?"

"OK, OK!" Mrs. Scott conceded. "But we have to be extra careful. Do exactly what your instructors tell you. Juniors can do the ropes course, while Brownies can use the treetop rope swing."

As the four friends waited their turns, Ella called them into a huddle. "I found something," she said.

"Where?" Avery asked.

"In the tree knot," Ella replied.

"Well, what is it?" Pari asked, unable to hide her impatience.

"I haven't looked yet," Ella said, pulling the rolled orange slip of paper from her pocket. "It may be nothing, but at least it's the same color as the last one. That's a good sign."

Ella smoothed the scroll and read the scrawled note:

I think some Girl Scouts
took the box we've been
using. The 10 p.m. X 4,
C-1 went off without
a hitch. No sign of the
witch.

—S.

Beneath the words, in very different
handwriting, was a response:

Good. If the
witch gets too
nosy, make sure she
disappears.
Tonight 6 p.m.
X 3, C-2. Be on
lookout!

—T.

Got it!
—S.

19

ON THE ROPES

"Avery, Ella, Pari, Kiara!" Mrs. Scott called. "The ropes instructor is ready to put on your gear!"

The fog was slowly dissipating as the girls donned their safety harnesses and helmets that would protect them in case they fell.

"The ropes are damp and slick," the instructor warned as she clipped each of them to the safety line. "Take your time, but have fun!"

Avery and Pari decided to help the Brownies on the rope swing before tackling the ropes course. Mrs. Scott had named Pari to be Ella's buddy.

Ella started her climb up to the rope swing. "Whew, it's kinda high up here," she mumbled. When she had almost reached the platform, her foot slipped abruptly. Ella's leg dangled back and forth like a pendulum.

"Ella!" Avery screamed.

"I've got her!" Pari yelled, standing right behind Ella. She wrapped her arms around Ella and secured Ella's feet on the platform.

"Thanks!" Ella said, looking a little pale. She gave Pari a bear hug.

"What are sisters for?" Pari asked.

Soon, Ella and Kiara had conquered their fear of heights and enjoyed several turns at the rope swing. Avery and Pari headed for the ropes course, and they breezed through the first few obstacles.

Next, the girls climbed a cargo net to the next platform, which was even higher in the trees. The fog had finally lifted enough to see most of the camp. "I see our campfire circle!" Avery said.

"And way over there you can see the lake," Pari added.

But something else caught Avery's eye—a big green truck with high wooden sides parked beside a trail.

"Whose truck is that?" Avery asked the ropes instructor stationed on the platform.

"Oh, that's Sam's truck," she answered. "He's the camp maintenance guy."

"Sam starts with 'S'," Avery whispered to Pari. "Just like the note!"

"Is he a super tall guy with blue eyes?" Avery asked the instructor.

"Yes," she answered. "Did you meet him?"

"I think so," Avery answered.

"Does he have a partner?" Pari asked.

"I don't think so," the instructor answered.

"I wonder what he's doing," Avery said.

"He's probably just clearing fallen branches off the trails," the instructor replied. "I wish he would work on the trails that lead to those hills over there. I've heard there are caves in them. I'm studying geology in college and I'm a spelunker."

"I thought you were a Girl Scout," Pari said, puzzled, "not a spunker."

The instructor laughed. "I am a Girl Scout," she said. "But I'm also a spelunker—that's someone who explores caves."

"Caves..." Avery said. "Hmmm, 'caves' starts with 'c'."

"I'm glad you're a good speller," Pari remarked, "but we have more pressing things going on here."

Avery and Pari finished the ropes course and met Ella and Kiara at the final obstacle. Avery grabbed Ella's sleeve and pulled her close to whisper in her ear. "Both the notes mentioned 'c' and a number. Maybe the 'c' stands for cave!"

"Good thinking, Avery," Ella said. "That idea is definitely worth checking out."

The ropes instructor they had been talking to joined the girls. She looked closely at Avery and Ella. "Are you related to Christina?"

"We're her cousins," Ella answered.

"I thought so," she said. "Christina told me her cousins were here. I see the resemblance. I'm Christina's friend Rachel."

"Rachel," Avery said, "I wish we could explore a cave!"

"Yeah!" Ella agreed, although not quite sure what her sister had in mind.

"I'm not sure we could even get to them," Rachel said. "Plus, I've got to stay on the ropes course until this afternoon."

The girls' faces fell. "Awwww," Avery complained. "It would be so educational."

"OK, OK," Rachel said. "I'm not making any promises, but let me talk to Mrs. Scott about taking you girls on a hike to look for a cave. Maybe we can even get Christina to go with us. Now, you better finish the ropes course. I've got more girls who need to use this platform!"

The girls made their way across a rope bridge. "Hold on tight!" Kiara warned as she bounced up and down, making waves in the bridge. "Stop!" Ella begged between giggles. "You're making me seasick!"

Ella and Kiara moved to a bench to watch the older girls on the zipline. They'd heard squeals and yells from this part of the course all morning and couldn't wait to watch the excitement.

"I'll go first," Avery volunteered bravely. Once she was safely harnessed in, the instructor said, "OK, you're ready to go!"

"WHEEEEEEEEEE!" Avery screeched as she zipped down the line at breakneck speed, her blond pigtails flying in the breeze.

Pari was next. After being harnessed in, she stalled for a minute to check her ponytail and take a deep breath. "I can do this, I can do this," she whispered. "WHOOOOOAAAAAAA!" Pari cried as she zipped down the line. Her brunette ponytail twirled behind her like a helicopter blade.

Ella and Kiara laughed as the girls sped down the zipline. "I can't wait until we are old enough to do that," Kiara said. "I feel the need for speed!"

CRACK! CRUNCH! Suddenly, Ella heard the sound of twigs breaking in the woods behind them. She turned to see what was causing all the noise. Her heart jumped as she saw a figure with a gray bun creeping through the trees. She grabbed Kiara's arm, digging her fingernails into her skin. "Witch!" she cried in a loud whisper. "It's the witch!"

20

DEAD END

"I'm not sure I want to go traipsing around to look for caves when a witch seems to show up wherever we go," Pari said, as the girls made the final stitches in new sit-upons during craft time.

"I know!" Kiara said. "It's too creepy!"

"We haven't heard from Rachel anyway," Avery said.

"Looks like we're at a dead-end with our mystery," Ella said.

"Oooo!" Kiara said and shivered. "Don't say dead!"

The girls had just finished their conversation when Rachel jogged up to their craft table.

"I have awesome news!" she said. "Mrs. Scott said it was OK for me to take you to the hills nearby. Christina is meeting us there."

"We're going now?" Avery said.

"Yes!" Rachel said. "Get your flashlights, everybody. We'll need them."

After the girls gathered their gear, they set off for the hills. The sun played hide and seek as they walked, peeking over the trees, then ducking behind them to cast shadows that looked like jail bars on the trail.

"The sun's going down fast," Kiara said.

"Yeah, I don't want to explore caves in the dark," Pari said.

"But it's always dark in caves," Rachel said. "That's why we have our flashlights."

After they'd walked a long way, Avery glanced nervously at her phone. "It's 5:30 p.m.," she whispered to Ella.

Ella nodded. "The last note said to be on the lookout at 6 p.m."

Finally, as the dusty pink of dusk deepened to dark purple, the trail ended abruptly near the foot of the hills. "Where do we go from here?" Avery asked Rachel.

"Another dead end," Ella said.

"Stop saying that!" Kiara cried.

"Christina said we'd meet at the trail's end," Rachel said, looking for Christina. "I saw a colony of bats flying from that area," she added, pointing at the base of a hill. "That probably means there is a cave nearby."

"B-b-bats?" Kiara asked. "I don't want to go in a cave full of bats!"

"They're not in there at night," Rachel said. "When it gets dark, they head out to hunt for insects."

"I wonder where Christina is," Avery remarked. "It's not like her to be late."

"I can't get phone reception here," Rachel said, looking down at her cell phone. "We passed a clearing a short ways back where my phone might work. I'll be right back. You girls wait here in case she shows up."

Avery glanced at her phone. "It's 5:50 p.m.," she said.

"Whoooo?" "Whoooo?" an owl cried.

"It's just us innocent little Girl Scouts," Kiara answered and giggled nervously.

"I hope that was an owl," Pari said, "and not the witch!"

Suddenly, the girls heard the low rumble of a truck engine in the distance. "Well, that's no owl!" Avery remarked.

"We'd better hide," Ella suggested.

The girls pushed their way through some brush, but to their surprise, the brush came right along with them.

"Are these tumbleweeds?" Kiara asked.

"No," Avery said, shining her light down a long, clear stretch of road. "Someone was hiding a road with fake bushes. And look here—these are the same tire tracks we saw last night!"

"Hurry! Hurry!" Ella warned. "The truck's getting closer!"

The girls broke into a run, following the road until it ended at the gaping mouth of a dark, damp cave.

21

SKULLS AND CROSSBONES

"Ooooooo!" Kiara cried, clapping her hands and jogging in place on her tiptoes. "I don't wanna go in there!"

"We don't have a choice!" Avery said. "There's nowhere else to go."

Kiara reluctantly followed as Avery, Ella, and Pari slowly entered the cave, anxiously looking in all directions. With a trembling voice, she sang the Brownie Smile Song to herself—over and over and over.

Outside, the girls heard a truck's growling engine suddenly stop.

"They must be coming!" Ella whispered.

But suddenly, the engine roared back to life, and they listened as the truck sped away.

"Hopefully we're safe now," Ella said.

"We'll wait a few minutes before we go back out," Avery suggested as she shined her light around the cave. "What's all this?" Her light illuminated a stack of gray metal storage barrels.

"Look at them," Ella remarked. "They have skulls and crossbones on them. Why would that be on there?"

"Maybe it's where the witch stores people before she changes them into other creatures," Kiara suggested. A shiver ran up her spine.

"Kiara! Don't say that!" Ella barked. She looked closely at the barrels. "Some of them must have been here a long time. The ones on the bottom are rusty."

Pari used her flashlight to trace the colorful rivulets coming from the barrels. "At least cave water is pretty!" she said.

Ella stepped even closer to the barrels and noticed that trash littered the ground around them. "Look!" she said. "I see more of those potato chip bags, like the ones under the cache tree and on the trail."

"We should have brought our garbage bags," Kiara said, shining her light on the trash. "We could have picked all of this up." She suddenly paused. "You guys! Look at that! That's my special cookie bag covered with hearts. How did it get in here?"

Ella walked over to the bag. She grabbed a grimy corner and lifted it carefully. When she did, she was shocked to see her sash smooshed in the dirt underneath it. "I don't believe it!" she said. "There's my sash! How in the world did it get in here?"

"Shhhhh!" Avery commanded.

"Wh-wh-what's that sound?" Ella asked, as a series of chirps, whistles, and low growls echoed in the cave.

"I was just thinking how this would make a perfect home for Tic-Lic," Pari said. "Let's get out of here, Avery!"

Avery shined her light into the darkness behind the barrels. She gasped as four sets of eyes glowed back at the girls. "Oh yeah, it's time to go!" she said.

As the four friends spun on their heels to run, a mother raccoon and three babies scurried past them in a big hurry. But then, the girls saw something much scarier between them and the cave entrance. It was the witch—and she had Rachel and Christina with her!

"Please don't turn us into lizards!" Kiara begged, eyeing the witch's metal box.

"What?" the woman asked, peering over gold-rimmed glasses. "What are you talking about?"

Although Avery's heart was pounding, she stood tall in front of the other girls. "You let my cousin and her friend go! Right now!" She held her cell phone high in the air. "Or I'll call the police!"

"Let us go?" Rachel asked. "I'm confused. Why are you saying that?"

"She's the witch!" Ella cried. "Get away from her!"

"Girls," Christina said, "calm down. This is Miss Carter. She's an environmental scientist, not a witch!"

"That's right," Miss Carter said. Her eyes darted over to the barrels leaking fluid near the girls' feet. She motioned the girls to move away from them.

"Girls, what you should be afraid of are those barrels," Miss Carter explained. She shined her flashlight on the "pretty colors" in the water Pari had spotted. "That liquid is poisonous! Now I know what's going on. These chemicals have been leaching into the ground and finding their way into the springs that feed the lake. They have polluted the lake!"

"And we've got a good idea who did it," Ella said. "Come with us. We have some interesting things to show you!"

22

COOKIES AND CRITTERS

Avery, Ella, Pari, and Kiara were dressed and ready for the final day's award ceremony. Ella had scrubbed her sash and hung it up to dry overnight. It was wrinkled, but Ella wore it with pride. She could see Mimi and Papa sitting proudly in the group of parents and grandparents there to see the ceremony and pick up their campers.

Miss Carter stood near the group of folding chairs where the Girl Scouts gathered for the ceremony. Mrs. Scott looked on proudly. "You girls look wonderful!" Miss Carter exclaimed. "And thanks to you girls, the mystery I've been working on for more than a year has finally been solved!"

"So, how did you finally solve your mystery?" Avery asked.

Miss Carter smiled. "We traced the barrels in the cave back to a nearby chemical factory. A man named Tom had a contract to haul their waste away."

"I bet Tom was the 'T' on the notes we showed you," Ella said.

"That's right," Christina said.

"Tom learned he could make a lot more money if he stuck the barrels in the cave without paying disposal fees at the hazardous waste dump," Miss Carter explained.

"Was Sam helping him?" Ella asked.

"I'm afraid so," Rachel said. "That's why when we saw him near the cave, he sped away in such a hurry."

"I'm sure he's also the person who had been leaving threatening notes for me," Miss Carter said. "He didn't like me snooping around the camp and collecting samples."

"Is that what you carried in the metal box?" Pari asked.

"Yes," Miss Carter replied. "I'm sorry you girls thought I was a witch," she added. "I've loved this camp since I was a Girl Scout and used to camp here. When people started noticing dead fish in the lake and asking where all the songbirds had gone, I knew the ecosystem was sick. But I didn't know why."

"So that's why I didn't hear any songbirds and why we found a frog with five legs!" Ella exclaimed.

"That's true," Miss Carter said. "But once the waste is cleaned up, the ecosystem will begin to heal. And who knows," she added with a wink, "maybe Tic-Lic will even come back to the lake!"

"Miss Carter, tell them about your special surprise," Christina said, beaming.

"You girls have done such a great thing for this ecosystem and this camp, I've nominated you all to receive Girl Scout safety awards," Miss Carter announced.

The girls lifted their hands and enthusiastically high-fived each other. "That's good news for our sashes," Ella said.

But her mood soon turned serious. "I still don't understand how my sash got into that cave," she added. "That's a mystery I still haven't solved."

"I'll tell you how," Rachel announced. "Remember that little raccoon family in the cave? I feel sure they took it, along with the bag of missing cookies. The weather will soon turn cold, and those raccoons were collecting food and making a den in the cave to stay warm. They probably dragged it from your tent."

Ella and Kiara looked at each other and nodded. "That makes total sense!" Ella exclaimed. "And I'll bet it was a raccoon I saw scratching at our tent the other night. The mama raccoon was coming back for more stuff!"

"I think you've figured it out," Miss Carter said. "That's good detective work."

Ella looked down at her freshly cleaned sash. "Thanks to those raccoons, we solved a big mystery while we were trying to solve a little one," she said. "You never know who or what is going to be the last piece of the mystery puzzle."

Ella turned to Avery and their two friends. "But best of all," she added while giving Pari a big hug, "I got a new big sister along the way!"

The End

About the Author

Carole Marsh is the Founder and CEO of Gallopade International, an award-winning, woman-owned family business founded in 1979 that publishes books and other materials intended to guide, inspire, and inform children of all ages. Marsh is best known for her children's mystery series called **Real Kids! Real Places! America's National Mystery Book Series.**

During her 30 years as a children's author, Marsh has been honored with several recognitions including Georgia Author of the Year and Communicator of the Year. She has also received the iParenting Award for Greatest Products, the Excellence in Education award, and been honored for Best Family Books by *Learning* Magazine. She is also the author of *Mary America, First Girl President of the United States,* winner of the 2012 Teacher's Choice Award for the Family from *Learning* Magazine.

For more information about Carole Marsh and Gallopade International, please visit www.gallopade.com.

TALK ABOUT IT!

1. At the beginning of the story, Ella was nervous about going camping because she was unsuccessful the first time she went. Have you ever failed at doing something but found the courage to try again? Give an example.

2. Ella was embarrassed when all the girls laughed at her when she mistakenly thought she had a leech on her cheek. Share your most embarrassing moment. How did you handle your embarrassment?

3. The Girl Scouts in the mystery had heard a story about a creature named Tic-Lic that lived in the lake. What's your favorite scary story? Why do you like it?

4. In the story, someone is unjustly accused of stealing. Have you ever accused someone

of doing something, and then found out you were wrong? How did you apologize? Why is it important to apologize?

5. At the beginning of the camping trip, Ella and Pari don't get along, but in the end they become good friends. Has there ever been anyone you thought you didn't like who later became your friend? How did you get past your differences?

6. The girls enjoyed cooking their food over the campfire. If you have been camping, what is your favorite campfire food? What do you enjoy most about cooking outside?

7. In the story, the girls help uncover the source of some environmental pollution. Why are trash and pollution harmful to the environment? What can you do to fight this problem?

8. What was the scariest part of this mystery? What was the funniest part of the story? Who is your favorite character, and why?

BRING IT TO LIFE!

Book Club Activities for a Class or Girl Scout Troop

1. S'mores have been around at least since the 1920s when the recipe was published in the first Girl Scout handbook. Create your own s'mores recipe by adding some new ingredients! Have a tasting party around the campfire or fireplace.

2. Tic-Lic was a legendary creature in the book. Create your own creature on heavy card stock. Decorate it with glitter, feathers, yarn, or any other art supplies you have available. Punch a couple of holes in the top of your art, tie a ribbon through it, and hang it on your wall.

3. Use colorful vinyl tablecloths to make sit-upons for your troop. Add a hook to attach your sit-upon to your backpack. Remember to take it on your next hike to use during a rest stop.

4. Copy Pari's idea and recycle old socks to make headbands, wrist bands, and ponytail holders. The more colorful you can make your items, the better!

5. Use a shoebox to make a diorama of a camp you would like to visit. Include tents, a campfire, a lake, canoes, a ropes course, or anything else you'd like to have there. Don't forget to name your camp.

6. Ask an adult to help you make hobo dinners with your troop. Include your favorite meat and vegetables in your heavy-duty aluminum foil package. If you don't have a campfire, you can use the oven!

SCAVENGER HUNT!

Let's go on a Scavenger Hunt! See if you can find the items below related to the mystery, and then write the page number where you found each one. *(Teachers and Girl Scout Leaders: You have permission to reproduce this page for your students/Girl Scouts.)*

_____ 1. A pillowcase

_____ 2. A butterfly

_____ 3. Garbage bags

_____ 4. A green roasting stick

_____ 5. A troll doll

_____ 6. Bacon in a bag

_____ 7. Lemonade

_____ 8. A yellow sock

_____ 9. Flying bats

_____10. Nail polish

GIRL SCOUT GLOSSARY

ADVISOR
An adult volunteer who works with Girl Scout troops or interest groups at the Cadette level and beyond

AMBASSADOR
A Girl Scout in Grades 11-12

BASIC OUTDOOR SKILLS
Skills learned by Girl Scouts to prepare them for outdoor activities

BROWNIE
A Girl Scout in Grades 2-3

BROWNIE RING
A circle formed by members of a Girl Scout Brownie troop for discussing troop business and planning activities

CADETTE
A Girl Scout in Grades 6-8

COUNCIL
Throughout the country, the Girl Scout organization is divided into councils that are chartered by the national organization. Councils serve specific geographic areas.

COURT OF AWARDS
A ceremony where girls receive awards for their achievements

DAISY
A Girl Scout in kindergarten or Grade 1

GIRL-ADULT RATIO
A safety practice of having a specific number of adults present among a given number of Girl Scouts

GIRL SCOUT BIRTHDAY
March 12, the official birthday of Girl Scouting, marks the first meeting of a Girl Scout troop in 1912

GIRL SCOUT GOLD AWARD
The highest award in Girl Scouting that recognizes the leadership, efforts, and impact girls have had on their communities

GIRL SCOUT HANDSHAKE
A formal way of greeting other Girl Scouts and Girl Guides, where girls shake hands with the left hand and give the Girl Scout sign with the right hand

GIRL SCOUT SLOGAN
"Do a good turn daily."

GSUSA
Girl Scouts of the United States of America

INSIGNIA
Overall term for Girl Scout earned grade-level awards, religious and other awards, emblems, and participation patches and pins

JULIETTE GORDON LOW
Founder of the Girl Scouts of the United States of America (GSUSA); her nickname was Daisy

JUNIOR
A Girl Scout in Grades 4-5

KAPER CHART
A chart or wheel showing the job assigned to each girl or group of girls for a project; often used at meetings, campouts, and special events

LEARNING PETALS
Awards earned by Girl Scout Daisies; each petal is a different color and represents one of the ten parts of the Girl Scout Law

MIMINAL-IMPACT CAMPING
Camping where the physical landscape of the campsite is preserved and the camper leaves no trace of activity at the site

NATIONAL HEADQUARTERS
The Girl Scout national organization's center of operations in New York City

PATROL
A small group of girls that plans and carries out activities within the troop or larger group

PATROL LEADER
A leader elected or appointed to head a troop/group patrol

QUIET SIGN
A traditional technique for obtaining silence at all Girl Scout meetings, made by raising the right hand; group members raise their hands and become quiet until complete silence is established.

REDEDICATION CEREMONY
A ceremony where Girl Scouts renew their Promise and review what the Girl Scout Law means to them

RESIDENT CAMP
A local Girl Scout-sponsored camp where girls attend for a week or more, or stay overnight

TROOP/GROUP CAMPING
A camping experience of 24 or more hours that is planned by a Girl Scout troop with its leaders and advisors

SENIOR
A Girl Scout in Grades 9-10

Enjoy this exciting excerpt from:

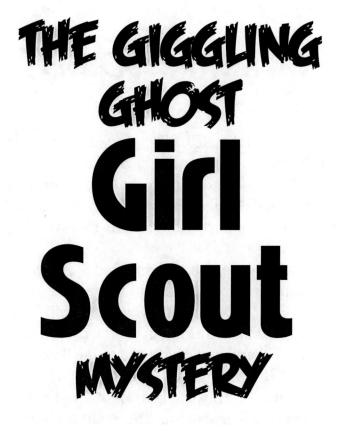

THE GIGGLING GHOST Girl Scout MYSTERY

1

SAVANNAH BOUND!

BLAM!! SPLAT!! Grant burst into Christina's bedroom like a mini-tornado and nosedived straight onto her bed, scattering neatly piled clothes. He sprang up and started bouncing; his unruly blond hair swooshed up and down.

"I'm going on a shrimp boat! I'm going on a shrimp boat!" he sang.

THUMP! Christina's backpack fell off the bed. Her khaki Girl Scout sash, covered with brightly colored metal pins, slid to the floor.

"GRANT!" yelled Christina. "What are you doing?" Her stick-straight brown hair flipped into her eyes as she spun around to stare at him. "I'm packing for Savannah! Now you've messed up everything!"

Grant back-flipped from the bed into the middle of the room. His cousins, Ella and Avery, giggled uncontrollably. Christina's two friends, Grace and Amber, tried to hold back their laughter. Christina's brown eyes glared at her little brother.

Avery tugged Christina's arm. "Come on, Christina. I'll help you pick up things."

"Do a good turn daily!" said Ella, jumping up to help. "What's a shrimp boat, Grant?" she asked.

"Papa says it's a boat that goes out and catches shrimp!" replied Grant. "We're going to Tie-Bee Island." He looked puzzled. "I wonder how you tie a bee—do you use thread?"

Christina giggled. "You mean *Tybee Island*, Grant," she corrected. "It's an island just east of Savannah."

"That sounds like fun!" said Grace. She plucked Christina's sash from the floor. "Look at all these badges and pins you have!" Grace began to jive around the room. "I'm so happy to be going to Savannah!" she sang. "I can't wait for the Girl Scout Camporee! And we have three whole days to see Savannah before it even begins!"

The girls were headed to the National Girl Scout Camporee at Fort Stewart, just a few miles from Savannah. It was the 100th anniversary of the founding of the Girl Scouts, and the Camporee was going to be a spectacular event this year. Girls from all over the United States were coming to Savannah.

Christina, Grant, Ella, and Avery's grandparents, Mimi and Papa, had a home in the lovely old historic district of Savannah. Mimi had invited everyone to stay there for a few days. They could explore Savannah before the big event began later in the week.

"I love Savannah!" said Amber, her brown eyes twinkling. "I went there with my troop when I was younger. It was in the spring, and flowers were blooming everywhere. It was beautiful!"

Each of the girls was at a different level of scouting. Tiny, blond, blue-eyed Ella was a Daisy. Her cheerleader sister, Avery, was a Brownie. Grace was a Junior Girl Scout, and Amber was a Cadette. Christina, the oldest of the group, was a Senior Girl Scout.

"I have to finish my summer honors history project on General James Oglethorpe while we are there," Christina told the girls. "He was the founder of Savannah. I have a lot of research to do, but I can show you around the town. And you can do some things on your own! There will be tons of girls there. I'm happy Mimi can take some time away from her writing and take us to Savannah. She says she needs a vacation!"

Mimi was the well-known children's mystery writer, Carole Marsh. Since Christina and Grant were older than their cousins, they often traveled with Mimi and Papa when Mimi researched her mystery books.

"Every time you go somewhere with Mimi, there's some kind of spooky mystery!" exclaimed Avery. "Isn't that how she gets all her ideas for the mystery books she writes?"

"Not this time," insisted Christina, patting her younger cousin's arm. "We have other things to do—and this trip is purely for fun! *No mysteries allowed!*"

As Christina closed her suitcase, her grandmother breezed into the room.

"Is everyone ready?" she asked, her shiny gold earrings swinging around her short, sassy, blond hair. "Papa's in the van and is ready to hit the road! Does anyone know where Grant is?"

"He was just here, Mimi," said Ella, throwing her little arms around Mimi.

Everyone looked around the bedroom.

"Yes, he was!" said Christina. "He just tornadoed my bed!"

Suddenly, Grant popped up from behind a chair. He clutched a box of mint cookies. His mouth was stuffed full, and chocolate cookie crumbs clung to his chin.

"Where did you get those?" cried Christina.

"Beshide urr bd," mumbled Grant, chewing. He gulped. "Beside your bed!"

Christina grabbed the empty cookie box and peered inside. "Empty!"

"Don't worry!" said Mimi. "There are plenty more where those came from. Let's go to Savannah!"